A Note to Parents

Rhyme, Repetition, and Reading are 3 R's that make learning fun for your child. **Rhyme Time Readers** will introduce your child to the sounds of language, providing the foundation for reading success.

Rhyme

Children learn to listen and to speak before they learn to read. When you read this book, you are helping your child connect spoken language to written language. This increased awareness of sound helps your child with phonics and other important reading skills. While reading this book, encourage your child to identify the rhyming words on each page.

Repetition

Rhyme Time Readers have stories that your child will ask you to read over and over again. The words will become memorable due to frequent readings. To keep it fresh, take turns reading, and encourage your child to chime in on the rhyming words.

Reading

Someday your child will be reading this book to you, as learning sounds leads to reading words and finally to reading stories like this one. I hope this book makes reading together a special experience.

Have fun and take the time to let your child read and rhyme.

Francie Alexander

—Chief Education Officer,
Scholastic's Learning Ventures

For Elizabeth Anne Lewison,
my egg-straordinary daughter
—W.C.L.

To Roberta Lou,
many thanks for the eggcellent support
—D.Z.

ISBN: 0-439-33407-1

Text copyright © 2002 by Wendy Cheyette Lewison.
Illustrations copyright © 2002 by Debra Ziss.
All rights reserved. Published by Scholastic Inc.
SCHOLASTIC, RHYME TIME READERS, CARTWHEEL BOOKS, and associated logos are trademarks and/or registered trademarks of Scholastic Inc.

Library of Congress Cataloging-in-Publication Data

Lewison, Wendy Cheyette.
　　Little Chick's Happy Easter / by Wendy Cheyette Lewison; illustrated by Debra Ziss.
　　　　p.　cm.— (Rhyme time readers)
　　Summary: Rhyming text describes Little Chick's Easter surprise for his mother.
　　ISBN 0-439-33407-1
　　[1. Chickens — Fiction. 2. Animals — Infancy — Fiction. 3. Easter — fiction.
　　4. Eggs — Fiction. 5. Stories in rhyme.] I. Ziss, Debra, ill. II. Series.
　　PZ8.3.L592 Li 2002
　　E — dc21   2001040016

10　9　8　7　6　5　4　3　2　1   02　03　04　05　06

Printed in the U.S.A.　　24
First printing, March 2002

· RHYME · TIME · READERS ·

Little Chick's Happy Easter

by Wendy Cheyette Lewison

Illustrated by Debra Ziss

SCHOLASTIC INC. Cartwheel B·O·O·K·S ®

New York   Toronto   London   Auckland   Sydney
Mexico City   New Delhi   Hong Kong   Buenos Aires

april

S	M	T	W	T	F	S
		1	2	3	4	5	6
7	8	9	10	11	12	13
14	15	16	17	18	19	20
21	22	23	24	25	26	27
28	29	30				

Easter!

Little Chick wakes up one day.
He sees that Easter is
on its way.

"I'll give Mama
an Easter surprise!
But what will it be?"
Little Chick sighs.

"*Cluck, cluck, cluck!*"
says Mama Hen.
"I will be back
at half past ten."

Little Chick sees the eggs
and then . . .

"*Peep, peep, peep,*"
says Little Chick.
"Mama is gone . . .

I must be quick!"

He rolls each egg
out of the nest.

Maybe a basket
would be best.

"*Moo, moo, moo,*"
says Mrs. Cow.
"What is Little Chick
up to now?"

Into the workshop
goes Little Chick.

Soon he's done.

Quick, quick, quick!
Back to the hen house
he goes again.

Just in time
for Mama Hen.

Little Chick says,
"Surprise, surprise!"
Mama can't
believe her eyes.

"How pretty!"
she says.
"You are a dear!"
Then all of a sudden,
what do they hear?

"*Peck, peck, peck!*"
Then what do they see?

The eggs are hatching—
one, two, three!
Now *Mama Hen*
has an Easter surprise.
And Little Chick
can't believe *his* eyes!

This Easter surprise is
like no other.
Two little
sisters

and one little
brother!